Kite Flying

markers

sandpaper

paper

bamboo

small saw

craft knife

joining tubes

metal rings

Kite Flying

Grace Lin

Dragonfly Books · New York

Visit us on the Web! www.randomhouse.com/kids

Educators and librarians, for a variety of teaching tools, visit us at www.randomhouse.com/teachers

Library of Congress Cataloging-in-Publication Data
Lin, Grace.
Kite Flying / Grace Lin.
   p. cm.
Summary: A girl describes how her family makes and flies a kite.
ISBN 978-0-375-81520-1 (trade) — ISBN 978-0-375-91520-8 (lib. bdg.) — ISBN 978-0-553-11254-2 (pbk.)
1. Kites—Juvenile literature. [1. Kites.] I. Title.
TL759 .L54 2002
629.133'32—dc21
2001033456

MANUFACTURED IN CHINA

17

To my dad and the King Kong kite we flew when I was a kid.

The wind is blowing.

It is a good day for kites.

Ma-Ma joins
sticks together.

Ba-Ba glues the paper.

Mei-Mei cuts whiskers.

Jie-Jie paints a laughing mouth.

I add
dragon eyes.

We all help attach the noisemaker.

Dragon, are
you ready to fly?

Look up!
Our dragon is talking to the wind!

What do you think
he is saying?

Many people believe that kite flying began in China over 2,000 years ago. The ancient Chinese believed that kites could carry away their bad luck and talk to the spirits in the sky. While the first kites were probably rectangular, elaborate kites of dragons, birds, and insects were eventually constructed from bamboo and paper or silk, each shape symbolizing traits that the person flying the kite wished to possess. The dragon kite, for example, symbolizes wealth, wisdom, and power.

People also attached bamboo strips to their kites so that the kites would make a ringing noise when flown. This noise was similar to the sound made by the *zheng,* a Chinese stringed instrument. The Chinese word for kite is *feng zheng,* meaning "wind *zheng.*"

Flying kites has become a cherished pastime. The annual kite-flying festival is held on the ninth day of the ninth month and is now sometimes referred to as "the Double-Nine Festival." Traditionally, however, the festival was called *Teng Kao,* which is translated literally as "ascending high," because people had to climb to high ground in order to fly their kites.

Kite flying soon spread to other countries. Japan, Thailand, and India all have their own kite traditions, with different festivals, customs, ceremonies, and legends. For example, in Thailand during the month of March, an annual "kite-fighting" tournament is held.

The Western world has also been much involved with the kite, even using it for weather forecasting, flight, and radio. Many people are familiar with Benjamin Franklin's electrical experiments during thunderstorms using a metal key and a kite, but few people know that a kite helped to build the bridge over the Niagara Gorge between the United States and Canada!

But now the kite is mainly flown for fun. The styles and materials have changed, but adults and children all over the world enjoy flying kites—an ancient and modern pleasure.

industry

wisdom

repels bad magic

summer

love

faithfulness

joy

abundance

long life

peace